▶ **Bugs in Your Ears**

BETTY BATES

▶ Bugs in Your Ears

HOLIDAY HOUSE
New York

Copyright © 1977 by Betty Bates
All rights reserved
Printed in the United States of America

Library of Congress Cataloging in Publication Data

Bates, Betty, 1921–
  Bugs in your ears.

  SUMMARY: Disappointed because she dislikes the man her mother marries, Carrie has difficulty adjusting until she realizes that her step brothers and sister are also having difficulty adjusting.
  [1. Remarriage—Fiction. 2. Adoption—Fiction]
I. Title.
PZ7.B29452Bu   [Fic]   77-3821
ISBN 0-8234-0304-1

▶ FOR TED, MY FAVORITE DAD OF ALL

▶ CONTENTS

1 Our Place 11
2 Dominic's Kids 23
3 Stepmother 37
4 Newton 43
5 Ginger 59
6 Rick 75
7 Mom 89
8 Dominic 105
9 The Family 115

▶ Bugs in Your Ears

1 ▶ OUR PLACE

It's Thursday night, so naturally Mom and I are having tuna fish. She's got three different ways of fixing it. Tuna fish casserole, tuna fish with hard-boiled eggs, and tuna fish salad.

I hate them all.

Tonight it's the casserole, which isn't quite as horrible as the others. There's strawberry ripple ice cream for dessert. No cookies, because we're all out, and Mom already spent this week's grocery money, and anyway she won't have time to shop till her day off next Wednesday. See, she works for this ear, nose, and throat doctor every day but Wednesday and Sunday.

"Anyway," she says, scooping up a smashed strawberry, "we don't need cookies. Dr. Muldoon says they haven't got all that much food value."

Sometimes I can't stand Dr. Muldoon.

After dinner Mom washes the dishes and sticks them in the drainer. Meanwhile I'm taking the breakfast dishes out of the drainer and putting them on the table, so I got to work fast to keep ahead so I don't get jabbed with a fork.

"Carrie," says Mom, sticking the plastic cups upside down in the drainer, "you baby-sitting tomorrow?"

"Yeah. In the morning. Over at the Zimmermans'."

"Okay, so on your way home you can stop at the hardware store and get screws for the bathroom soap dish."

"Do I have to, Mom? Peg's coming over for lunch."

Peg's my best friend. We're both going into eighth grade next month.

"Yes, you have to. Peg can come a little later, and maybe you'll have a little less time to listen to that what's his name, that disk jockey that says, 'How's everybody everywhere today?'"

"Y'mean he says, 'Hi, evvverybody. How's evvverybody evvverywhere today-yay?' It's really neat the way he says today-yay. Sort of runs it all together, y'know?"

Mom laughs, and I've got to laugh too. I mean, the way her face lights up when she laughs, and her mouth gets all wide and happy, you can't help laughing with her. She reaches over and musses my hair with that teeny hand of hers with the soapsuds all over it. It feels good, but I make this face anyway. I mean, soapsuds!

Mom has to depend on me lots of times, so I say, "Okay, I'll go to the store. Anyway, I've got to go to the dime store sometime and get a notebook for school, and lined paper."

Mom pushes the curl up off her forehead with her arm. "Listen, take the soap dish with you so you can tell the screw size, and get the money out of my save-up box. If they don't have the right-sized screws, see if Mr. Flugum has some. I hate for you to bother him, but we've just got to get this place organized."

We've lived here almost eight years, ever since we moved into this apartment of Mr. Flugum's when I was four. He lives under us, on the second floor, and his plumbing shop is on the first floor, which makes it nice when we need a plumber. But still, after all this time, the hem is still down on one of our bedroom curtains, and the bathroom rug is still ripped, and the soap dish in the bathroom is still off the wall, and one of the legs on the coffee table in the living room still needs gluing. Mom just never gets time to fool with stuff like that.

Sometimes I wish my dad was still around. Mom kicked him out when I was maybe a year old. He drank, she says. She tried to help him quit, but he wouldn't. Maybe. But maybe if he was still around he'd fix the soap dish and the wobbly leg on the coffee table.

That evening we're in the living room watching this detective show on TV, and Mom's mending one of her white uniforms, and I'm writing my grandma in Florida to tell her which plane to meet when I go down to visit her next Tuesday. In the show, this blond is about to get poisoned at a party, and I'm glad Mom's with me. I guess it's silly, but I still get scared sometimes. I bet if my dad was here I'd never be the tiniest bit scared. Peg says she never gets scared, and maybe it's because she's got her dad at home. He's tall and skinny, and he can play *On Top of Old Smoky* on the mouth organ. I mean, I'd never even know about mouth organs if it wasn't for

Peg's dad. Anyway, Mom's here now, and it makes me mad when the phone rings and she goes in the bedroom and answers. I bet it's Dominic.

I can't stand Dominic.

My mom is dating him. She's got this habit of dating men she meets in Dr. Muldoon's office. There was this department store detective and this newspaper reporter named Buck and this bandage salesman from out of town who, she found out later, had a wife and six kids. She met Dominic when Dr. Muldoon moved to a bigger office on the twenty-first floor of his building last January. Dominic was one of the moving men. He's got three kids and no wife. He's short, with hairy arms and thick sideburns and black eyebrows, and—well, he actually does sort of scare me somehow.

I'm right. It's Dominic on the phone. I can tell because Mom talks low, as if she doesn't want me to hear. She's been doing that lately with Dominic. Something's going on between those two, and I don't like it. I keep on writing my letter, jabbing the pencil down on the paper. On TV, the blond has been poisoned, and she's lying on the floor dead surrounded by excited people talking, with her hair flopped in all directions and the glass fallen out of her hand and ice cubes all over the carpet, and Mom's talking louder now. "Tomorrow'd be just fine, Dominic. Gino's? Sure. You know I love lasagna."

She does not love lasagna. She likes it okay, but she doesn't actually love it. How come she said that? I mean, she's going out with this man with enormous muscles, and the blond girl on TV is still lying on the floor dead while the people talk, and the ice cubes have got to be melting all over the carpet, and tomorrow night I'm going to have to stay home alone without any mom or any dad.

The commercial comes on. It's for this mouthwash. Some guy named Ron has lost his girl because he doesn't use it.

Mom hangs up and comes and sits down. On TV, Ron's girl is finally letting him kiss her because he started using the mouthwash. I'm still jabbing the paper with my pencil, and Mom gives me this long, long look. "What's the matter, honey? You mad at me?"

"'Course I'm not."

"Sure you are. You're mad because I'm going out with Dominic tomorrow night."

"Well, he always smells like garlic. He oughta use

that mouthwash."

I bet my dad wouldn't go around smelling like garlic all the time. I keep saying this to Mom over and over. We talk about Dominic a lot, and how I feel about him, but I never seem to be able to make her understand.

Mom sighs. "Maybe I should have him to dinner sometime so you can really get to know him."

"C'mon, Mom. What would you want to do that for?"

"Come to think of it, maybe I wouldn't. Back when I asked Buck for dinner, I caught you jabbing your heel into his ankle under the table."

"Well, I was a lot littler then."

She doesn't say anything. Just keeps on sewing for a minute. Then, "Y'know, Carrie," she says, "you can't always have me all to yourself."

The TV show comes on again, and now the police are there, all yelling at each other, so I don't have to think about what she just said.

When Dominic shows up the next evening, he's all dressed up in this brown sports jacket and pants. I mean, he's this big brown blob from his hair and sideburns on down. He smiles at me. The smile is white. "Hi, Carrie. Your mom here?"

Well, what did he expect? "Sure, she's here. She'll be ready in a minute."

He doesn't smell like garlic, but naturally he will after he eats lasagna. So will Mom.

"You gonna ask me in?"

"Oh, yeah. Sure."

I open the door wider. It comes to me that he hasn't got any neck. I mean, his head sits right on top of his shoulders. He takes up about half the living room. He just stands there like some great big teddy bear that doesn't know what to do with its hands. "So you're gonna go visit your grandma, hey, Carrie?"

"Yeah."

"And then you're gonna be in eighth grade?"

"Yeah." Some question!

"My Newton's going into eighth. He gets pretty good grades. Your mom says you get pretty good grades too."

"Uh huh. They're okay."

There's this long pause. Finally Mom comes out of the bedroom, thank goodness. "Carrie, you might've asked Dominic to sit down."

"Oh, yeah. I forgot."

Well, I didn't exactly forget.

Dominic smiles at Mom in this revolting way, so his teeth look all shiny. "Say, you look good, Marie."

She's got on this pale blue size seven dress that she got at a sale. It seems to light up her face somehow. There's this curl that falls down onto her forehead just right and matches those big brown eyes of hers. She smiles back at Dominic. It's kind of as if they've got some deep secret that I don't know about, and I get this sort of sick feeling.

After a while Dominic turns and looks at me. "You gonna be okay by yourself, Carrie?"

"Sure, I'll be okay."

Mom squeezes my arm. "Put the chain on the door, honey."

Dominic pats me on the head—I mean, he really does actually pat me on the head—and then they're gone.

I put the chain on the door.

That night I only watch fun shows. But still, I keep thinking about that girl getting poisoned, and that spoils the whole thing. I can't even go and get a cookie to make me feel better because there aren't any, and that makes me mad. I'm kind of mad at Mom anyway, because Peg and I fixed the bathroom soap dish, and Mom didn't even say thanks. She must have noticed.

Around ten I go to bed. I keep falling asleep and waking up, falling asleep and waking up, staring at Mom's empty bed and wondering when she's coming home. I'm positive it'll be never. Funny. For some silly reason, I reach over and touch my treasure box on the table between my bed and Mom's. It's this wooden box with a secret panel for opening it, and I keep my special things in it. Like the stub from the ticket to *Our Town,* the play Mom took me to at the high school. My grandma gave me the treasure box when I was little. Somehow it makes me feel safer to touch it, and after a while I pick it up and set it beside the pillow and just keep my fingers on it.

Finally there's the sound of the front door opening, and voices. It's Mom and Dominic all right. There's this long silence. Guess he's kissing her good-night. Yuck! The front door closes, and then Mom's in the bedroom doorway. She's this teeny shadow, with the living room light behind her. Very slowly the shadow drifts in and sits on my bed and smooths the sheet that's already smooth. What's going on, anyway?

"You awake, Carrie?"

"Yeah." I can smell the garlic.

She reaches out and musses my hair. She musses and musses. How come she keeps doing that in the middle of the night?

Finally she leans down and puts her cheek tight against mine and holds me close to her. Her cheek is wet. "Honey," she says, "I have to tell you. Dominic and I are getting married in October."

2 ▶ DOMINIC'S KIDS

Sometimes everything goes all wrong. I mean, here I am trapped into having Dominic for my new dad, and who needs a dad with black eyebrows? Maybe I can talk Mom out of it. Except I've got only three days to do it in before I go visit Grandma.

I don't have any luck, of course. Mom won't budge. She keeps telling me to remember to pack my bathing suit and to be sure and help Grandma with the dishes and not to lose my ticket. Boy-oh-boy, does that make me mad!

Visiting Grandma is okay. I'm crazy about her. She never talks about her arthritis the way some of her friends do. The awful part is that after I get back

I'm going to have to get used to Dominic, and I'm going to have to get to know his kids. Ricardo, Ginevra, and Newton. What kind of crazy names are those?

The wedding's going to be the last Saturday in October, and then Mom and Dominic are going up north to some resort for about eight days. So Mom tells Mr. Flugum we're moving out by the first of November, and he says he really will miss us, but it just happens that his daughter and her husband are looking for an apartment, so everything will work out fine because they can have ours.

Everything's working out fine for everybody but me.

Grandma lives in Apartment 10-T of this huge, air-conditioned apartment building with a lot of other old ladies in it, and some old men, who wander back and forth between each other's apartments for coffee and lunch and cocktails. They all make this big fuss over me before they start talking about their arthritis. It's more fun being alone with Grandma. She tells me she likes the way my hair curls down onto my neck now, and that I don't need to worry about the pimples on my forehead. They hardly show. She asks me nonstop questions about

Mom and Peg and Mr. Flugum, and about baby-sitting the Zimmerman kids, and about Dominic. She especially asks me about Dominic.

A couple of times she takes me to the beach and sits on this bench and knits. She wears this big wide straw hat and sunglasses that take up half her face, and this bright blue slack suit. She looks like some Munchkin out of the *The Wizard of Oz.* It's really hot, and there's hardly anybody around, and the sand burns my feet, but it's fun playing in the waves. I wish I could swim, though.

On the way home I say, "Do you know how to swim, Grandma?"

"I never learned, honey. If you ever get a chance to learn, you grab it. You never know when you'll be on a boat that tips over and dumps you in the water so you've got to swim around and hang onto it." She turns and looks at me through the Munchkin sunglasses. "You got to be ready for everything in this world, honey."

She's absolutely right.

At supper that night I don't feel so good. Grandma squints at me over her yogurt and coffee. "Honey, what happened to you? You're all splotchy."

"C'mon, Grandma, I am not."

"I'm not kidding. I think you've got chicken pox."

"I already had chicken pox."

"Well, something's the matter with you. I'm taking you to see Fritz."

"Who's Fritz?"

"A doctor that lives in the building. Used to be a foot doctor in Stroudsburg, Pennsylvania. He takes care of all of us."

Fritz is down one floor in Apartment 9-J. He's about as wide as a straw. He leans on his cane and feels my forehead and my neck. When I say "Ouch," he says, "She's got German measles. She'll run a fever for two or three days, and then she'll be fine. Keep her inside."

Actually I'm not all that sorry he said that. I'm feeling hot and cold at the same time, and my knees are like paper.

The next morning while I'm lying around reading about ostriches in Grandma's encyclopedia, Mom calls. Mr. Flugum's daughter and her husband need the apartment on the first of September, so she has to move out all of a sudden. "I'm going to move in with Dominic," she says.

Holy Columbus! "Y'mean you're going to—um—sleep with him?"

"Uh huh. We're getting married tomorrow."

"Mom! You can't do that."

"We don't want to just sleep with each other, honey. We want to get married first. That's the way we feel about each other."

I've got to admit I'd rather have them get married. I don't go for this business of my mom sleeping with some man she's not married to. So here I am absolutely helpless, feeling like some kind of drippy wet sponge, and my mom is about to marry this man I can't stand. What am I going to do?

"Maybe I can get there, Mom. Maybe I can do it."

Grandma yells from the kitchen. "No, you can't, Carrie Mills. I'm not putting you on a plane in your condition."

"Dja hear that, Mom?"

"Uh huh. What did she mean by your condition?"

"German measles, Mom. I got spots all over me."

"Oh, Carrie!" There's this long pause. "Well, of course you can't come. And I wanted you to get to know Dominic's kids before we got married. Listen, let me say hello to Grandma, will you?"

"Sure. 'Bye, Mom."

"'Bye, Carrie. I didn't want it to happen this way. But anyway you'll be able to start school with

Newton. That's going to be nice."

Sure. It'll be great. I'll be going home to a different apartment that won't even be home, and I'll be going to school with some creep named Newton.

After the spots go away, I'm still pretty gloomy. I think about Mom off in that resort with Dominic. She's probably not even worrying about me. I mean, things are never going to be the same again between her and me. Grandma takes me to the beach, but I don't feel like fooling around in the waves. I just sit on the bench with Grandma and watch her knit. "Carrie," she says, "you're homesick, aren't you, honey?"

"How can I be homesick? I haven't even got a home."

"You're homesick for your mom."

"Well—um—I, maybe."

"Listen, I'm going to send you back. I'm going to get ahold of her at that resort and tell her she and Dominic have got to cut their honeymoon short and meet you at the plane and take you to the new apartment."

"But I don't want to go to the new apartment."

She sets her knitting down and puts her tubby

little arm around me tight. "I know you don't . But you don't want to stay here either. You belong with your new family."

I got to admit this idea makes me feel better. I do want to see Mom more than anything, and I'm not all that unhappy about cutting that honeymoon short.

After supper Grandma calls Mom at the resort and tells her I'm taking the next plane back, and I start packing. While I'm cramming my bathing suit into my slippers, Grandma opens her bureau drawer. She takes something out and drops it into my hand. "It's for your treasure box. Something I've saved since I was about your age."

It's this round thing that looks like some kind of medal. I never saw a thing like that before. "It's a silver dollar," says Grandma. "They don't make them any more, so it's kind of like a souvenir. I guess you could say it's a souvenir of my childhood. Maybe it'll bring you luck."

"Thanks, Grandma. Hey, thanks a lot."

I'm going to keep it forever. To remember her by.

The plane doesn't get in till almost midnight. Mom and Dominic are there. They just barely made it to the airport. Mom hugs me, and all of a sudden I feel tired. Mom and Dominic put me in the back seat of Dominic's car so I can lie down. "Listen, honey," says Mom, "you'll have to sleep on the sofa bed in the living room till Dominic gets your bed set up. Everything's happening too fast. We left that hotel in such a rush I forgot to pack my slippers."

"We didn't even have time to call my kids," says Dominic. "Boy, are they gonna be surprised!"

Yeah. They'll be surprised all right. I guess I don't feel as good as I thought I did. I close my eyes and go to sleep.

Pretty soon I wake up. Dominic's picking me up. He carries me up some stairs and plunks me under some covers and whispers to me. "Now listen, Carrie, if my kids come in here tomorrow morning and wanna know what you're doing here, you tell 'em to go knock on our bedroom door and ask us. You got that?"

"Mm." I nod with my eyes closed.

I hear footsteps tiptoeing out of the room and down a hall somewhere. I guess Mom and Dominic think I'm asleep, and I guess I am, almost.

The next morning when I wake up I feel human again, until I start to remember. Yeah, I'm still in the sofa bed. I close my eyes and then open them again slowly. It's for real. I'm in this living room that's got to be Dominic's. There's this jacket draped over the back of a chair and this book lying open in the middle of the floor and an apple sitting on the TV set. No sign of Mom or Dominic, of course. I know enough about life to know they're going to sleep late. After all, they're still on their honeymoon. And when those kids get up and see me here, what are they going to say? I mean, we haven't even been introduced yet.

They'll probably hate me.

Well, Dominic told me what to do, so I'm going to do it.

Footsteps. Ooh boy! Somebody's coming.

It's this boy with big ears. The elastic in his pajama bottoms is loose, and his stomach sticks out. He looks about my age. He's got something in his hand.

Well, here goes. "Hi," I say. "I bet you're Newton."

"Yeah." He stares at me through these enormous glasses.

Oops! That's a dead fish he's holding. "Hey, Newton, what're you doing with that—um—thing?"

"Feeding my boa constrictor. Got to get him ready for the science fair at Paulson Park today."

"Oh. Well, if you wanna know why I'm here go ask your dad."

"Yeah? Well, I'm busy, so quit bugging me."

What's going on with him? There's this perfect stranger in his living room, and all he can say is "quit bugging me."

He turns on the TV. It's one of those cartoon shows. Some cat is chasing some mouse. Newton shuffles over to the aquarium on top of the bookcase. His pajama bottoms are ready to fall down any second. I can hardly look. He lifts the screen that's across the top of the aquarium and sticks the fish down inside. This wiggly gray and brown thing snaps it up.

What kind of a weird place is this anyway? A boa constrictor. I don't even know how to spell it.

More footsteps. Somebody else is coming.

"Hey, Newton, whadja do with my soccer ball?" There's the somebody else, almost filling up the doorway. He's got on this T-shirt with wrinkles all over it and HIFFLICKER HIGH HORNETS in big letters across the front.

"Hi," I say. "You gotta be Ricardo."

"Yeah."

"Well, if you wanna know why I'm here—"

"Hey, Newton, where's my soccer ball? I got pre-season practice this morning, y'know."

He's deaf. He's got to be deaf.

"C'mon, Rick," says Newton. "How come I always gotta keep track of your dumb old ball? Anyway, it's behind the sofa bed."

Rick is not deaf. He moves the sofa bed, with me in it. He grabs the ball and tosses it in the air. I duck. He catches the ball over my head. "Coach Boone's gonna really look us guys over today. Hope I make first-team goalie. You coming to watch, Newton?"

"Nope. I'm taking Frederick to the science fair. I'm giving this demonstration on how I taught Frederick to eat dead fish instead of live mice."

Yuck!

The cat in the cartoon is now being chased by a dog, but nobody's watching. The phone rings, but Newton's busy cleaning Frederick's cage and Rick is kicking the ball around the floor lamp and I'm not about to answer their stupid old phone.

After a while Rick yells, "Answer the phone, Ginger. It's probably for you." This door on the other side of the room opens, and this girl with red hair comes out. She's about fourteen, maybe. "What's the matter with you guys? Can't you answer the phone?" She answers the phone, and she giggles a lot.

In the cartoon, there's this bear chasing the dog.

Finally the girl hangs up. Ginger. Short for Ginevra, I guess. Maybe she'll listen to me. "Hi, Ginger," I say in this loud voice.

"Oh, hi," she says without looking at me. "Boy, am I starving!" She picks up the apple from the TV set and dusts it off. She flops into this chair and bites a big hole in the apple.

What kind of a crazy family is this anyway? Nobody listens. I thought they'd hate me. Well, they don't hate me. They don't even know I'm here. I can't stand moving into a dumb place like this.

I'm going to do something about it.

I jump out of the sofa bed and run over and turn off the TV right smack in the bear's jaws. "Now you listen, everybody." I'm yelling. I mean, I'm really yelling. "This is important, so pay attention. Last night your dad and my mom brought me here. I'm your new sister Carrie, and I'm moving in."

Rick quits practicing kicks and stares.

Newton quits cleaning the cage and stares.

Ginger stops chewing and stares. "You're kidding."

"Nope. It's so. I don't like it one bit, but it's so. They're here now, in a bedroom somewhere."

"But they're not supposed to come home till Monday," says Rick.

"Well, they're here."

"So how come you didn't say so before?"

"I did say so, but you wouldn't listen."

"Y'mean," says Newton, "y'mean your mom is our new mom?"

"She's not our mom," says Ginger. "She's our stepmother."

Newton swallows so his Adam's apple bobs down and up. "Stepmother." He says it as if he's saying boiled cabbage. "So I suppose from now on we gotta do what she says."

Ginger takes a bite of apple and chews. "'Course not. She's not our real mom."

I don't like her saying that, one bit. That's my mom she's talking about. "Listen, she's really okay. She says funny things lots of time. And—and she can cook. She makes great fried chicken and hot dogs and—um—tuna fish casserole."

Rick wrinkles his nose. "Tuna fish casserole. Yuck!"

Sounds as if they like my mom about as much as I like Dominic. They've all got these gloomy looks on their faces.

Ginger swallows. "Boy-oh-boy, is that ever a dirty trick Dad played on us, getting married like that! And I thought you were some science freak friend of Newton's spending the night on account of the science fair."

"I thought you were some friend of Ginger's," says Rick.

"So did I," says Newton, grabbing his pajama bottoms, thank goodness.

"You guys are really something else," I say. "You all got bugs in your ears."

"Hey, we got bugs in our ears." Rick starts swatting his ears and making faces as if he's got bugs inside his head, and we all start laughing, maybe to keep from crying. We laugh harder and harder, and pretty soon we're all hanging onto our sides. All except Newton, who's busy hanging onto his pajama bottoms.

3 ▶ STEPMOTHER

After a while Rick goes off to soccer practice and Newton goes to the science fair and Ginger takes off to see her friend Mindy that she just talked to on the phone. That leaves me all alone, so I call up Peg. "Peg, I'm never gonna see you again."

"Whadya mean you're never gonna see me again? You nuts, Carrie?"

"Nope. See, my mom married Dominic early. She had to get out of our apartment while I was gone, so all of a sudden she married Dominic."

There's this awful silence. In the background there's the sound of Peg's dad playing *On Top of Old Smoky*. I never knew the words, but they must be sad.

"Are you still there, Peg?"

"Yeah. Yeah, I'm here."

"So I'm over at Dominic's, and of course I gotta go to this other school now."

"Carrie, it's awful. It's just awful."

"Yeah. Peg, I wanna see you again. I'll call you again." I don't know what to say next. Peg and I used to have so much to talk about, but now I can't think of anything more to say.

"I'm gonna miss you, Carrie."

"Yeah. Me too. I mean, I'll miss you too."

"Promise you'll come see me?"

"Sure. I promise."

The mouth organ is playing the last note of the song, long and drawn out like this sort of wail.

I don't think I can ever keep that promise. I don't think I ever can see Peg again. I couldn't stand it.

"'Bye, Peg," I say real fast.

"'Bye, Carrie."

I hang up.

Everybody's there for lunch, including Mom and Dominic, who were up around ten looking dreamy. Dominic brings two extra chairs, and we all crowd around the kitchen table. "We're gonna have to do something about this table," says Dominic. "It's too crowded."

"It sure is," says Rick in this sarcastic voice.

Mom's playing with her watch, so I know she's nervous. "Awright," says Dominic, "you kids are gonna be nice to your new mom."

They all nod and start shoveling in the food.

The baked beans taste like mud in my mouth. Rick, next to me, knocks me with his elbow reaching for the bread. Newton, on the other side, moves his chair away from me as far as he can, which is about half an inch.

"What's everybody been doing this morning?" says Mom.

Why doesn't somebody say something?

Finally I say, "I called Peg. I had to tell her—um—the news."

"Mmm. What did you do, Newton?"

"Science fair."

"I've never seen a science fair," says Mom. "What's it like?"

"Aw, nothin'. Just this bunch of people milling around." He crams bread in his mouth and mumbles, "Boy, do I hate baked beans!"

Under the table, Rick steps on my foot. It feels like a ton of cement. "Ouch! Get your big foot off mine."

Ginger giggles.

"Oh, sorry," says Rick. "It's so crowded here I can't help it." He's pressing down really hard now.

"Well, get it off anyway." I pinch his leg.

He moves the foot. "Hey, quit it. Whadya mean by pinching me, ya little brat?"

"I said get your foot off, didn't I?" I jab his ankle with my heel. Nobody gets away with that kind of stuff with me.

"Will ya cut that out?" says Rick.

Dominic pounds on the table. "Awright, awright. You kids leave each other alone."

"But he deliberately—"

"I don't care. You just stay away from him."

"But Dominic," says Mom, who's at the counter dishing out applesauce, "he had his foot on top of hers. I could see—"

"Listen, all I did was—"

"But she jabbed him right in the—"

Dominic pounds the table again. "Shut up everybody. You want the neighbors calling the police? Everybody be nice and quiet. Listen, you kids, Carrie's got a lot to learn 'cause she's new here. So you teach her how to act nice."

"She already knows that," says Mom, plunking two dishes of applesauce on the table.

"She already knows tha-yet," says Ginger in this silly high voice.

Newton giggles.

Holy Columbus! What's the matter with Dominic and his kids? They're really goofy.

"Awright," says Dominic. "Nobody says another word. Eat your applesauce and get out of here."

Everybody shuts up and eats like crazy, including me.

"When you're through," says Mom in this loud voice that sounds really mad, "everybody bring your dishes to the sink and scrape them. Carrie and I'll do the dishes today. Tomorrow, Dominic and Ginger, and then Rick and Newton. Then we start over."

Everybody stares, including me. All of a sudden Mom's laying down the law. Maybe because she's got to. Because there's no other way for this mess to get taken care of.

"Hey, how come we still gotta do all the work?" says Rick.

"Yeah," says Newton. "How come?"

Ginger takes her gum out from under the table and sticks it in her mouth. "If she thinks she's gonna get away with that—"

"You do it," yells Dominic. "You do what she says, ya hear?"

He's finally got some sense after all.

Everybody does it, including Dominic. But his kids do it real slowly, and all the time they're looking at my mom sideways, as if she's some kind of poisonous spider, and just before Ginger goes out of the room, she turns around and sticks her tongue out.

I despise this place.

4 ▶ NEWTON

After the breakfast table gets cleared off the next morning, Dominic picks it up. I mean, there he is in the kitchen holding this table as if it's a piece of cardboard. The muscles in his arms are sticking out all over, and he's got this big frown all over his face.

Mom stares. "Hey, Dominic, what are you doing?"

"I'm getting rid a this thing. I'm throwing it out. I never wanna see it again." He stomps out the back door, and we can hear him clomping down the outside stairs.

Mom goes to the door and yells. "But what are we going to eat off of?"

"I'll get a bigger one," he yells back. "My boss has got one."

Sure enough. After he and Ginger do the breakfast dishes, he drives over to the moving company and comes back with this enormous table with a top that looks about half the size of the kitchen. "It's okay," he says. "Somebody stored it and left it behind. The boss said I could have it any time."

Dominic and Rick start moving things out of Ginger's room so they can set up my bed in there. Dominic's muscles are sweating. Ginger and Newton are in there emptying bureau drawers for me, and Mom and I are working in the living room. My treasure box is at the top of one of the cartons, so I take it out and stick it on top of the bookcase so I can unpack some books. In the bedroom, Ginger says in this loud voice, "I could be sleeping late. Nobody ever lets me sleep late."

"I didn't have time to feed Frederick," says Newton. "He'll starve."

Well, I didn't ask them to fix up the room. Dominic did. How come they're so mad? What about me? I'm the one who's got to move. I grab some books out of the carton and swing around fast, knocking my treasure box off the bookcase. There it lies, with the panels and its insides scattered all over the floor. My treasure box.

I just don't think I can stand it.

Mom comes up behind me. "Oh, Carrie, what happened?"

"It—it fell. Oh, Mom, it's all busted. Oh, Mom!" I can feel the tears running down my cheeks. I must be crying.

Mom puts her arm around my shoulders. "It's okay, Carrie. Dominic can fix it. He'll glue it back together, and you won't even know the difference."

"Dominic!" I spit out that name Dominic.

"But, Carrie, he likes you, honey."

"Then how come he didn't stick up for me yesterday? How come he had to go and tell everybody I got a lot to learn?"

"He hardly knows you, honey. Listen, I know it's tough, but it'll get better when we all get to know each other."

"I don't wanna get to know that family."

"Listen, Dominic's going to adopt you. He's going to give you his name. Then it'll be your family too."

"But I don't want to be a member of that family. All we do is fight with each other. Anyway, I don't want that crummy name Ginetti. I—I want my own name." I wipe my nose with my wrist. "Anyhow, Dominic drinks. You told me my dad drank. Well,

Dominic drinks too. That night he had to wait for you, when you were going to the fights. That night he had a beer while he was waiting."

"Oh, Carrie, he doesn't drink the way your dad used to. It's different."

"No, it's not different. It's not. Anyway, he sweats. Dominic sweats."

Mom gives this big sigh and pats me on the shoulder and says very quietly, "Pick up the pieces, Carrie. It's going to be okay."

Sure. Everything's going to be just great. Dominic's going to adopt me, and I don't want to think about it, so I'm just not going to.

The next day is Labor Day, and the day after that is Tuesday, the first day of school. Rick and Ginger leave early for high school. Newton and I make sandwiches and take the bus to school. My stomach's turning over because I don't exactly know what to expect, and I miss Peg and the rest of the kids at my old school. I mean, I didn't even get a chance to say good-bye, except to Peg.

At school, the principal assigns me to Mrs. Holbrecher. That's Newton's teacher. With five eighth grades, how come I get assigned to Newton's room?

I join Newton in the hall outside Room 248, where this bunch of kids is waiting. He looks away, trying to pretend he doesn't know me, but that doesn't fool the other kids.

"Hey, Newton, who's your friend? Who's the girl?"

"Screwy Newy's got a gir-ull."

Some of the guys are grinning at us. They're all bigger than Newton. He's the skinniest guy around.

"Aw, shut up." Newton turns his back on them and scrunches up his shoulders.

Screwy Newy. What kind of a dumb nickname is that? "Do they call you that all the time?" I say.

"Call me what?"

"Screwy Newy."

"Naw. Not all the time. Anyway, I don't care." His voice is kind of shaky.

He cares.

Somebody opens the classroom door, and we crowd in. Maybe they put me with Newton on purpose because he needs protection. I don't like the way things are going for him. I mean, he's revolting, of course, but I am stuck with him.

Mrs. Holbrecher closes the door and sits down with her flabby arms on the desk in front of her. She blinks at me, and I give her the piece of paper the principal gave me. Her bracelets jingle when she takes it. "Carolyn Mills?"

"Yes."

"All right, Carolyn, we're happy to have you with us. You can take the seat in the row next to the window. The fifth seat back." She nods that way, and her blond curls bob. The color looks fake.

Newton's in the row next to the door, way across the room. Second seat back, behind the biggest guy in the class. Wouldn't you know?

In front of me is this tall, skinny guy I heard somebody call Mike. Across the aisle is this girl with long hair the color of peanut shells who smiles at me. "Hey, how come you came with Newton?" she says.

"He's my—um—stepbrother." Actually I'm sort of ashamed of Newton. Who wants to be hooked up with a guy who gets called Screwy Newy? Especially if his last name is Ginetti. I mean, why should I give up a perfectly good name like Mills? "I'm Carrie Mills," I tell the girl. "See, my mom married Newton's dad very suddenly."

"Wow, is that ever romantic! Aren't you excited?"

"Well—um—sort of."

"I'm Heather," she says, running her fingers through the peanut shells. "Heather Grasky. Nothing that exciting ever happens to me."

"Welcome back, class," says Mrs. Holbrecher in this siren-type voice. "I know we're going to have another good year together, a very exciting year."

This little giggle goes around the classroom, but she ignores it. She starts introducing the new kids, two boys and three girls, including me. When it's my turn, everybody turns and looks, and I feel myself turn red. After that Mrs. Holbrecher gets Mike to pass out the math books, and when he gets to me he gives me this big grin that's all teeth.

"All right, class," says Mrs. Holbrecher. "All right, settle down." We're reviewing fractions. Mrs. Holbrecher keeps writing things on the board and asking questions, and Newton keeps raising his hand. "All right, class, what are three-fourths plus one-eighth? Yes, Newton."

"Seven-eighths," says Newton in this bored voice, as if he's trying to pretend it's the easiest thing in the world.

"That's right, Newton. Now explain it to the class, please."

Hardly anybody else is raising a hand, but Mrs. Holbrecher calls on some other people anyway. This tubby guy by the name of Stafford gets a lot of the answers. But Newton keeps waving his hand like some big red flag. No wonder they call him Screwy Newy. He's trying to hog the whole thing.

For social studies and English we file down the hall to another room. Outside the door, Heather whispers in my ear, "Wait'll you see Mr. Shramm, Carrie. He's weird."

Mr. Shramm's got this long, skinny neck and long, skinny fingers. He reminds me of one of those lampposts that bend at the top. "I want you all to read the section on America before Columbus," he says, with his head sticking out in front of his shoulders. "Let's imagine we were here five hundred years ago. What was it like?" Somebody giggles, but he ignores it. He looks around the room with this smile that reaches almost to his ears.

In my other school, I read a book on American history last spring for supplementary reading, so it's not all new to me. After a while Mr. Shramm tells us to close our books. "Now, class, did we get the feel of the place and time? What did we learn?" Naturally Newton's hand is raised. Naturally he wants to be the whole show.

It ends up with Mr. Shramm and Newton having this big discussion about native American tribes all by themselves. Holy Columbus! How come Newton doesn't shut up? Mike turns toward me and grins and says out of the side of his mouth, "Screwy Newy, the brain."

Poor Newton!

Finally Mr. Shramm looks at the clock. "Now, for English, we're going to write a descriptive story. Adjectives," he says, waving his hands in the air. "Make them work for you. Make each one sing."

Mike giggles.

I think and think, and finally I write about the bears and seals and monkeys Mom and I saw when we went to the zoo one time. I use adjectives like rugged and sleek and agile.

We get to read ahead in our history books while Mr. Shramm looks over our stories, and after a while he asks Heather to come up and read her story about a trip she took with her dad and mom and brother to the mountains, in which she talks about the burning sunset over the pines. When she gets back to her seat, I say, "That was really nice, Heather."

She smiles so this dimple shows in her left cheek.

It's lunchtime. In the cafeteria, Heather leads me

to this table of girls from our room, with Stafford sitting alone at one end. He's eating this sandwich, and he's got two more in front of him, plus chocolate cupcakes. No wonder he's fat.

One of the girls looks at me sideways. "So you're Newton's sister," she says.

"Stepsister."

At another table Newton is sitting by himself at one end with his legs twisted around the front legs of his chair. At the other end of the table, Mike and the big guy who sits in front of Newton and a couple of other guys are laughing and chewing and slapping the table and ignoring Newton.

Poor Newton!

After school Heather asks me to go swimming at the Y Saturday morning. I remember what Grandma said about tippy boats, so I say yes, I'll go.

In the bus on the way home, Newton starts talking about Plymouth Colony. "Did ya know the Pilgrims really started out in two ships? One of 'em had troubles, and they all had to turn back, so that's how come—"

"Newton, you bore me. You really do bore me."

He blinks.

"You always gotta prove how much you know."

"Well, if I know it, then I oughta say it. Why

shouldn't I get credit for it?"

"I bet some of the other kids know things too. Maybe they need to get called on. Anyway, you gotta give 'em a chance."

"Why should I give 'em a chance? It's their problem, not mine."

"Listen, Newton, I know you know a lot. And furthermore I know all about the Mayflower and the Speedwell."

His eyes open wide. "Hey, how come you didn't raise your hand in class? I mean, if you know all that kinda stuff how come you didn't—"

"Well, for one thing, I gotta get used to things first. And for another thing, the teachers are gonna find out soon enough how much I know. I got nothing to prove." I don't tell him I read that history book.

He doesn't say much the rest of the way home. He looks out of the window. I feel sorry for him. I bet he misses his mom. Wonder what happened to his mom. Funny. I never wondered that before.

In math the next day Newton doesn't raise his hand. He just sits there staring at his thumbnail. Guess he decided to take my advice after all. Mrs. Holbrecher looks kind of surprised. Stafford raises his hand and answers a couple of questions, and so do Heather and I. Once she calls on Mike, and it turns out he knows the answer, and so does the boy in front of Newton.

Mike turns around and says, "What happened to old Screwy?"

I just shrug.

It really is nice having somebody besides Newton speak up, but he is sort of overdoing the silence bit. That afternoon on the bus I say, "You're overdoing the silence bit, Newton."

"C'mon, Carrie. Why don't ya make up your mind what you think?" He notices the social studies book on my lap. "Hey, I forgot. Mr. Shramm wants us to start reading the chapter on the colonies. How's about lending me your book tonight? I left mine at school."

It's comforting to know that Newton makes mistakes sometimes. "Okay. It's my turn to help with the dishes, but after that I need it. I gotta have it by eight."

At two minutes after eight he brings the book into the bedroom I'm sharing with Ginger and slaps it on the bureau. "Here y'are, Carrie."

"Thanks, Newt."

He doesn't even blink when I call him Newt. I'm beginning to like him the tiniest bit now that he's not acting like Alexander Graham Bell. I open the book to the chapter on the colonies, and out falls this dead fish.

"Hey, Newt, you come back here."

His head shows up in the doorway. "Yeah?"

"What's with the dead fish in my book?"

"It's a bookmark, ya dummy."

"Well, get it out of here and give it to Fred."

"His name isn't Fred. It's Frederick."

"Honestly, Newton! How come you're making such a big fuss over a stupid name? I mean, how come you have to be so formal? Why don't you call him Freckles or something? Haven't you got any sense of humor?"

I throw the fish at him. He catches it, but he doesn't seem to know he's caught it because he's standing there looking dreamy. "Freckles. Well, I gotta admit it's not too bad. Sorta goes with his physique. I mean, those big spotty marks look kind of like freckles. Yeah, it's not too bad."

"Physique. Whadya mean physique? Snakes haven't got shoulders."

"Yeah, that's right. They sure don't." He giggles. What do you know? He's human after all. He's got this really nice giggle. Like water when it starts to boil. So I giggle back.

"Hey, Newton," I say, "how do you spell the boa in boa constrictor? We never had it in spelling."

"Just the way it sounds. B-o-a."

"Yeah. I thought maybe there was a *w* in there somewhere. Well, thanks, Newt. And after this you be careful with my book."

"Boy-oh-boy, are you picky! I didn't hurt your old book."

"No? All you did was wreck the binding with your stupid fish."

The binding isn't wrecked, but he makes me mad. How come a guy that can be so nice can turn around and be such a complete pain? He didn't even apologize.

On Thursday morning Mr. Shramm says, "Now, class, we'll write another creative story. Today I want you to stress verbs. Write about an incident that changed your life. Use action verbs, dynamic verbs, verbs that push the story along." He makes this great big sweeping motion with his arm.

I write about Mom marrying Dominic because that's the most life-changing thing that's ever happened to me. I tell about how I got to know Dominic's kids. I'm glad I found out how to spell boa constrictor. I use verbs like scare and hate and yell.

When it's almost lunchtime Mr. Shramm asks me to come up and read my story. Everybody stares at me all over again, and I could die. When I get to the part where I'm yelling at Rick and Ginger and Newton, I keep my head down. Finally I come to the end, where Newton is hanging onto his pajama bottoms, and the whole class starts laughing. I feel terrible. I should never have done that to him. He's in enough trouble already, and after all he is my stepbrother and he doesn't have any mom.

But for some crazy reason Newton is laughing too, right along with the class. The guy in front of him turns around and gives him this friendly bop on the shoulder, and Newton doubles over and keeps right on laughing.

When I get back to my seat, Mike turns around and gives me this very respectful look. My face feels all flushed, and I turn away and stare at this nail in the floor. "How about that?" says Mike. "I can just see old Newton hanging onto his pajama bottoms."

At least he didn't say Screwy Newy.

In the cafeteria at lunch, Stafford goes up to Newton. "Hey, Newt, dja see that math problem in tomorrow's lesson about the Girl Scouts selling all those cookies? See, when you take the price of each box and—" Next thing I know, Stafford and Newton are sitting together and trading sandwiches.

Mike and his friends are at the other end of the table. "Hey, Newt, how's your buddy the boa constrictor?" "You got any dead fish in your lunch bag?" "Hey, Newt, your pants are falling down."

Newton just swallows a bite off of Stafford's sandwich and gives them his boiling water giggle. Then he turns and starts talking to Stafford as if he's not the least bit bothered.

He's learning.

In the bus on the way home from school, he says, "Listen, Carrie, how come you had to go and mention my big ears in that story, huh?"

As I was thinking before, how come a guy that can be so nice can turn around and be such a complete pain?

5 ▶ GINGER

There's this picture on the bureau in the room I share with Ginger of this lady with red hair and green eyes and shiny orange lips. She's gorgeous.

"Who's that?" I ask.

"That?" says Ginger. "That's my mom."

"Where is your mom?"

"She died. She went to work one morning and never came back. Somebody cut in ahead of her on the expressway."

Ginger is standing in front of the bureau brushing her hair so it's like shiny pennies. She doesn't look sad or anything. Just blah. What's she thinking anyway?

"When did it happen?" I say.

"In the summer. Two years ago. More than two years ago." She slams the brush onto the bureau and checks out this freckle on her forehead.

Two years ago Ginger was in junior high. What if that happens to me?

A week ago yesterday I moved into Ginger's room. Now it's Sunday again. Sunday night. I'm sitting on my bed. Dominic and Rick had to take out Ginger's dresser to get the bed in, and she had to take her things out of half the drawers in the bureau and put them in with other things so there was room for my socks and underwear and summer stuff. The things from my treasure box I hid under the socks. Naturally, we share the closet.

Now Ginger stretches out on her bed and pops some gum into her mouth. She kicks off her shoes. One of them slides under my bed, but she doesn't seem to notice. Just starts writing in this little white book with a lock on it.

"You writing in your diary?"

"Yeah."

"What're you writing about?"

"My mom."

She's chewing the gum like crazy, her green eyes are all squinty, and she's writing as if she's digging a hole in the paper. Ooh boy! She can't stand us moving in like this. She can't stand my mom sleeping with her dad. She can't stand me taking half her drawers and closet and crowding the room so she can hardly turn around and bugging her about her mom. Well, what about me? I didn't ask to come here. I didn't ask to be sharing a room with her instead of Mom.

What's it like losing your mom anyway? Naturally I don't even remember my dad. I don't even know where he is. Mom never even bothered to keep track of him. He couldn't keep a job, she says, on account of the drinking. Well, so maybe he's actually gentle and kind anyway. Like Mr. March in *Little Women.*

I yank Ginger's shoe out from under my bed and stick it by her bed. She keeps on writing and snapping her gum. When she finishes, she fishes out this key that's hanging around her neck under her blouse. She locks the diary and sticks it under her mattress at the top of her bed.

I get into my bathrobe and wander out through the living room, where Mom and Dominic are watching some spy story. Mom and Dominic watching TV together. Seems funny. She's mending the lining of her brown coat, and he's gluing the leg on the coffee table we brought over. I don't like that. Dominic fixing our coffee table. But I guess I got to get used to things like that.

I scuff down the hall to the bathroom. Seems goofy to have to go through the living room every time I want to brush my teeth and—well—do all that stuff you do in the bathroom. I mean, what if somebody's got guests in the living room? Do I whiz through, or do I stop and say hello and ask if they've seen any good movies lately?

The bathroom door is closed. I turn the knob. "That you, Ginger?" says Rick's voice.

"Nope. It's Carrie."

"Oh—um—well, I'll be right out."

I lean against the wall. There's the sound of an electric razor. He's whistling. No wonder he's happy. He made first-string goalie on the varsity team.

The door bursts open, and he comes out wrapped in this towel, with his big chest sticking out. He makes me feel like some kind of midget. He stops whistling and looks at the floor all the way into the room he shares with Newton. Guess he's embarrassed because I'm not Ginger.

When I get through, Mom and Dominic are in their bedroom with the door closed. Ginger is

GINGER ▶ 63

watching TV in her bathrobe. In our bedroom, her shirt and jeans and socks and underwear are slopped all over my bed. "Hey, Ginger, your junk's all over my bed."

She doesn't answer, so I dump everything on the floor under her bed, where I've already dumped a lot of her stuff. When she comes to bed she says, "You didn't have to dump my stuff on the floor."

"You didn't have to dump it on my bed. So quit doing it."

She doesn't answer. But just before she turns over to go to sleep she whispers, "Brat!" I pretend to be asleep.

But I'm not. I've got this sick feeling, but I can't even cry. How can I cry with Ginger in the same room?

I keep finding her clothes on my bed, and her junk all over the top of the bureau. She's taking over the whole closet too. I keep having to push her clothes over. Nothing I say makes any difference. "Go tell your mom," she says. "Go on." Maybe I should tell Mom. But I won't. I'm no squealer. But I'd really love to take all her clothes and throw them in the incinerator, and I have to keep telling myself over and over, it's not easy to get a new mom and a new sister all of a sudden and have to share your room too. I guess I got to think about that.

On Saturday morning Dominic cleans the apartment. Mom's getting ready to go to work. She doesn't need to be there till ten. Rick's at his soccer game, and Newton's out buying dead fish. Ginger and her friend Mindy are in the living room working on their freshman poetry notebooks. I'm in our bedroom making my bed and waiting for Heather to pick me up again for swimming at the Y.

Dominic sings while he works. He vacuums down the hall and into the living room, and his voice sounds louder and louder. He's singing some song about a girl named Maria. Wow, can he sing! I got to admit he's got a great voice. The vacuum is pulling air in, and he's blowing it out, and he's winning. Maria. That's almost like Marie. Maybe he's singing about Mom, kind of. He comes by the door holding the vacuum close as if maybe he's dancing with it.

"Dad, for heaven's sake! We're trying to study," says Ginger's voice.

"Okay, okay, I'll sing soft." There's the sound of the vacuum going back and forth across the living room floor.

He's singing another verse, about kissing this girl named Maria, half as loud as he was before. But it's still pretty loud, and I'm humming along with him while I pull up my bedspread.

"Hi there, Carrie."

It's Dominic. All of a sudden he's standing there smiling at me from the bedroom doorway. He's got sweat all over his face, and he's breathing hard. All of a sudden I wonder if Mom ever gave him my treasure box to fix. Wonder if he's going to do anything about it. I know my own dad would. He'd fix it so the cracks would hardly show. But I bet Dominic doesn't care. I bet he threw the pieces away. Who wants a guy like that for a dad? Who wants to have the same name he's got?

Yesterday Mom told me we have a date to see a lawyer on October 12, along with Dominic. "We're going into court," she said. "We've got to go before a judge so Dominic can adopt you."

October 12. That's only about a month from now. I guess it's time for me to start thinking about it. But it won't do any good. There's nothing I can do to stop it, I guess.

Dominic's got the vacuum into the room. "Hi," he says again.

66 ▶ GINGER

"Um—hello."

"Say, how's about picking up your clothes so I can vacuum in here?"

"They're not mine." I don't say they're Ginger's. I wouldn't squeal. But I'm not going to get sucked into doing her job.

"They gotta be your clothes, Carrie. Ginger never leaves hers around. C'mon, pick 'em up."

"I told you. They're not mine."

He looks disgusted. "Hey, Ginger," he yells, "these your clothes on the floor under the bed here?"

"Carrie put 'em there."

"Okay, Carrie, pick 'em up." He comes farther into the room, and all of a sudden it looks extra crowded. He's got this big frown on his face, and his eyes are flashing. "Listen, Carrie, I don't wanna have to get mean to you."

Now I know he threw away the pieces.

"Listen, can't you see they're not mine? Honestly." My heart's pounding. I don't like to get nasty, especially to a guy as big and scary as Dominic. But I got to stick up for my rights. "Anyway, you're not my dad. You can't tell me what to do."

All of a sudden Mom walks in. "Carrie, I could hear your yelling all the way into the bathroom. What's the matter with you?"

Dominic wipes his forehead with the back of his hand. "This kid of yours, she won't pick up her clothes."

"Mom, they're not my clothes. He won't believe they're not mine. They're—" Oops! I almost squeal.

She doesn't say anything. Just stoops and picks up this pair of jeans. Underneath are a couple of green and yellow socks. Ginger's socks. "Look, Dominic," she says quietly.

"Ginger's. Wait'll I get my hands on—" He charges out into the living room. "They're gone. Ginger and Mindy, they're gone."

They must've left awfully fast. They must've gone to Mindy's.

He shakes his head. "Guess I should've known. But she used to be neat. She never used to throw stuff down like that. What's goin' on with her? That's some lowdown trick sneaking out like that. She's gotta pay for that."

"Maybe," says Mom, "she ought to vacuum the room when she gets back. After she picks up her clothes."

"Well—l, maybe," says Dominic. He's got lines in his forehead. He looks really sad.

"Sure, she's having trouble getting used to Carrie and me," says Mom. "But she's got to learn, Dominic. She's got to learn now."

He shrugs. "Okay, okay. She gets no dinner till she does it." He sets the vacuum behind the door, shaking his head. "How come my Ginger goes and pulls a trick like that? How come?"

At least he's got enough sense to worry about Ginger. That's something anyway.

The doorbell rings. It's Heather picking me up for swimming. She's carrying this little canvas bag. "You got your bathing suit, Carrie?"

"Uh huh."

After breakfast yesterday Mom gave me some money. "If you decide to join the Y, Carrie, you can join tomorrow. I'll pay for it. We're going to have more money now, with Dominic and me both working."

Mom makes pretty good money working for Dr. Muldoon. Plus she gets to bring home medicine and stuff for nothing. She learns things too. Like she's got these marvelous cures for corns and hiccups and stuff like that. She practices on me sometimes.

She was extra nice to me yesterday. Maybe she wanted to make up for the way she married Dominic all of a sudden. She must have been worrying about the way I hate this place. She put her hand on my shoulder and said, "There's extra money there for a bathing hat. You could get one after school today."

"Well, I do want to join. How come you're treating me extra nice, Mom?"

She gave me this kind of worried look. "You getting along okay?"

Rick came whizzing into the kitchen. "Hey, I got one minute to make my lunch. What's around for sandwiches?"

Mom opened the refrigerator door. "I got some baloney in here, Rick." She looked over her shoulder. "I'll talk to you later, Carrie."

She never has time for me any more.

Now, with Heather at the door, she says, "Maybe you could come back here for lunch, Heather."

Heather gives her that smile with the dimple in her left cheek. "Thanks, Mrs. Ginetti. Wish I could, but I got a baby-sitting job. Maybe next week I can."

The Y is a regular mob scene, just like last week. This big girl with her hair in a bun who taught me before makes me kick and move my arms in the water while Heather swims at the deep end with this bunch of other girls. A couple of them are from our school. Some of them are trying different dives. One girl even goes off the board backwards, and another one pretends to fall off, and everybody giggles. Looks like a lot of fun.

I'm the only one at the shallow end, and it's kind of embarrassing. The big girl gets me to try swimming from one side to the other, but it's hard to remember to kick while I'm lifting my arms out of the water and pushing them back in. I'm no athlete, for sure. Once I get a mouthful of water and think I'm going to choke to death, but the big girl pounds me on the back, and I'm okay. Anyway I'm better than last week, and maybe I'll get to the deep end one of these Saturdays.

Back in the locker room we have to shout on account of the place being so jammed. "Gonna join?" says Heather.

"Yeah, I guess so. The girl said I didn't do too badly."

"It'll be lots more fun when you get to the deep end."

Sure it will. And besides, I'll be with the others. That's what I really want. To be with the others.

When Heather leaves me at the door to our building, I ask if she wants to go to Rick's varsity soccer game with me after school on Friday. She says sure. I guess she likes me. It comes to me all of a sudden that my stomach's not turning over any more.

Ginger comes home late for dinner. We're all sitting around the kitchen table eating hot dogs. Dominic looks up from his beer. He starts to say something, but the words don't come out. How come he doesn't say something?

Mom looks up. "Ginger," she says, "you can have dinner after you put your clothes away and vacuum your room."

Ginger raises her eyebrows. "Whadya mean I can't have my dinner now? Listen, Dad, she can't tell me what to do. I don't have to do what she says." She pulls her chair out from the table.

Dominic swallows. "You do what she says. You go clean up that room real good." His voice is low and kind of fuzzy, but at least he finally got around to saying something. It's about time.

Ginger just stands there as if she can't believe he's really talking to her like that. Her eyes get all wet. She looks away and turns around slowly and walks out of the kitchen.

While she's gone, Mom makes her this special hot

dog with this thick piece of melted cheese in it. Ginger doesn't say anything when Mom gives it to her. Just takes the gum out of her mouth and sticks it under the table and eats the hot dog real slowly, sneaking looks at Mom between bites. Maybe she's trying to get used to her. Funny that anybody has to get used to my mom.

That night when we're in bed, Ginger writes in her diary for a long time. She's frowning. She must be writing awful things. Come to think of it, she must feel awful. It comes to me that she's really got problems. I mean, she lost her mom and everything, and now her dad's mad at her.

I take this deep breath. I've got to say it. There are some things you just got to say because maybe they might help. "I'm sorry, Ginger. I'm sorry your dad got mad at you. I'm sorry they had to move your dresser out of here."

She gives me that surprised look of hers, with her eyebrows up. "That's okay, kid," she says after a minute. "It's not your fault." She slips the diary under the mattress and drops the key inside her pajamas.

After that Mom has to remind her once in a while to pick up her clothes, and sometimes I do too. But mostly it's not so bad. Mostly she doesn't leave things around any more. Sometimes we even get to talking before we go to sleep. I tell her about my dad and how Mom kicked him out. We talk about all kinds of stuff. "Y'know, kid," she says, "you oughta wear red. How come you never wear it? You'd look good in red."

"Honestly?"

"Sure. With your light skin and your brown eyes and hair. I can't wear red, y'know. I gotta be careful what I wear, with my hair. Mom used to say—" She stops all of a sudden.

After a while I make myself say, "I'm sorry about your mom."

"Thanks, kid."

"You take my dad. I'd like to see him just once. And maybe talk to him a little."

"I know how you feel, kid. I feel the same about my mom. I'll never see her again, for sure."

We're quiet for a long time. Then she says, "Anyway, how come you're worrying about your dad? You gotta remember he was a drunk."

I get this sharp pain inside me, as if she's stuck me with a knife. A drunk. How can she turn around and say that right after she's been talking so nice?

I'm all mixed up.

6 ▶ RICK

After school on Friday Heather and I take a bus over to Rick's soccer game at his school. Hifflicker High against Penfield High. Newton can't come because he's got a dentist appointment, and Ginger's got a chorus rehearsal.

Rick told us at dinner last night that he's Hifflicker's only goalie today because the second-string goalie got caught smoking, and Coach Boone won't let him play. "He's a tough coach. He doesn't stand for any of that funny stuff."

At the game Heather and I sit on the grass near the bench, so I know Rick has got to see us. But he entirely ignores us. He walks around snapping his fingers and slapping the other guys on the back, so I guess he's either trying to exercise his muscles or he's trying to act tough because he's nervous. In fact, the whole team seems nervous. All those guys dressed in their underwear, kicking balls around, practicing before the game starts, and they're all snapping gum. Sounds like the Fourth of July.

I don't understand soccer at all. All those penalty kicks and throw-ins and stuff. All I know is that each team is supposed to get the ball into the other guys' net at one end of the field. That's the goal, and whoever does it gets one crummy point. And, boy-oh-boy, do they have to work hard to do that! They go tearing back and forth, back and forth, up and down the field. Arms and legs and heads are all tangled up with each other. Looks as if there'll be limbs all over the field when it's over. But they all end up attached to some body.

Rick's job is to guard Hifflicker's goal. He looks scary big standing there. Kind of like a gorilla with kneepads, only without all the hair. I mean, is this the kind of guy I want for my brother?

Once, when Penfield gets near our goal, Rick slips and falls making a save, and some sneaky Penfield kid with a beard comes roaring in and kicks the ball right over his kneepads into the goal. Poor Rick! He comes out of the first half huffing like some hurricane. He gallumps right by Heather and me and plunks himself on the grass behind us with the rest of the team. He stares down at his kneepads and takes the half an orange someone's passing out to all the guys. He looks as if he's in this deep, deep trance.

Coach Boone charges over to the team. His voice is hoarse from yelling. "Awright, you guys, we're behind. We gotta get going. Jackson, you're getting too many penalties. Quit hogging the ball. Pass it off to your wing. Morales, you gotta move, move, move. Action. I wanna see some action." He's waving his hands in the air, and he wants more action. Seems as if all we saw in the first half was action. "Ginetti, how many times I told you, stay with the goal. Don't go running out."

Rick sits with his legs crossed like some guru meditating, only he's chewing the edge of his orange. I mean, he's actually eating the skin. But he doesn't seem to know it. Coach Boone grabs his shoulder. "You okay, Ginetti?"

Rick nods very slowly. "Yeah, sure. I'm okay." He lets out this great big hiccup. I mean, it's absolutely enormous.

Everybody jumps.

"'Smatter, Ginetti, you got the hiccups?" says somebody.

"He's been hitting the bottle," says Morales.

Everybody laughs.

"Hic!"

Coach Boone's got these worried lines in his face. "You sure you're okay, Rick?" He's hoarser than ever.

"Sure I'm okay. I—hic—told ya. Sometimes I get hiccups when I'm nervous, that's all. Hic!" I think he's going to blow up.

Coach Boone sticks his arms around Rick's shoulders. "Ya gotta get a drink. C'mon over to the drinking fountain." He just about drags Rick over to the drinking fountain. Rick droops over the fountain like one of Newton's dead fish. Coach Boone turns the handle. Nothing comes out. "It's busted. The drinking fountain's busted." Coach Boone is yelling. He sounds like very rough sandpaper.

The hiccups are coming fast now. A dead fish with fast hiccups. "Get him another orange, for Lord's sake!" Coach Boone's pulling him toward the bench. The kid with the orange halves holds one out. Rick grabs it like a drowning man reaching for shore.

"Hic! Hic!"

Coach Boone paces back and forth with his hand on his forehead.

Jackson comes up behind Rick and yells, "Boo!" Rick just turns around and gives him this disgusted look and hiccups in his face and takes another swallow of orange.

"Two-minute warning," yells the referee.

"Hic!"

The orange isn't helping. Nothing's helping. Everybody's running around worse than when they're playing soccer, and Rick's sitting in the middle hiccuping with his face ketchup red. He looks smaller than he did before.

Morales taps him on the shoulder. "Hey, Ginetti, dja see that thing on TV last night? The one where they corner the murderer at the top of the Statue of Liberty and the guy has to fight him on that little balcony up there, and he falls—" His voice trails off. He's gotta be trying to get Rick's mind off his hiccups so they'll go away, but Rick is only staring into infinity and hiccuping like water going down the bathtub drain.

"This is awful," says Heather. I can't answer. I just sit there like some dead person. Rick's going to blow the whole game, for sure.

80 ▶ RICK

Coach Boone is looking around helplessly, probably for some magic cure. "Try holding your breath," somebody yells.

Rick holds his breath. There's this silence while everyone else seems to be holding their breath too. Suddenly this great big hiccup comes out of Rick. It sounds like Niagara Falls.

"One-minute warning."

Ooh boy! I can't look. I put my hands over my face and groan.

Hey, what's the matter with me? Holy Columbus, what's the matter with me? I'm so busy watching the show and groaning I forgot all about Mom's hiccup cure. I never tried it, but you can bet I'm going to now. Can I remember how she did it on me?

I get up and march over behind Rick. "I'll cure you, Rick. Get up."

"Huh?"

"I can cure you."

"You some kinda miracle worker, kid? Hic!"

"Yeah. Sure."

"G'wan. Go away."

Coach Boone is looking at me in this surprised way. But at least he doesn't chase me away.

"C'mon, Ginetti, get up. You heard her." He waves his hands in front of him. Guess he's ready to try anything.

Rick gets up slowly, as if he's going to get frisked. He looks around at the other guys. Somebody snickers, and Rick looks down at the grass. "Turn around," I say. He shrugs and turns around. "Now hold your breath and pull in your stomach." I grab him around the middle, above the waist, with both arms. I press in with my fingers like crazy. Yeah. That's the place. Right below where the ribs come together. He's got such an enormous chest it's all I can do to hang on. It's like hanging onto some St. Bernard.

Jackson laughs. "Hey, kids, this ain't the time or the place for that kinda thing."

"Quiet, Jackson." Coach Boone's voice is like walking on gravel.

"Okay, Rick," I say, "now let your stomach out."

I got to keep pressing that spot with my fingers while he lets his stomach out. My arms almost get pulled out of their sockets. I may explode. But I count to twenty before I let go. That should do the job.

"Hic!"

It didn't do the job.

"All right, everybody out on the field," says the ref.

I feel awful. Rick lets out this moan.

"C'mon, Ginetti," says Morales. "Quit makin' love, and let's get going."

Coach Boone stares at Rick and me. There's sweat on his upper lip. He's got to give me another chance. "Gimme another minute, Coach. I can do it."

Coach Boone wipes his forehead with his wrist. "Okay, guys, you gotta play without Rick. Get out there and keep that ball away from our goal if you bust your guts doing it. Fullbacks, play back, ya hear? You guard that goal till Rick gets in there." He turns to me. "Okay, kid, let's give it another try."

Rick's beginning to look groggy. His eyes are half closed. The hiccups must be wearing him out. I got to hurry.

Rick's got a chest like Fort Knox, but I manage to hang on even after he lets his muscles out. This time I'm going to count to thirty before I let go. I stick my head against his back, which is made of stone, and hold my arms around him till they ache. My fingers are ready to break. Meanwhile, the game's going on, and that ball's getting closer and closer to our goal. "Watch that goal, Morales," yells the coach in a whisper.

I'm up to ten.

Morales grits his teeth and stands with his feet apart. The ball goes right between his legs. I can't look. But I got to.

Our other fullback's there to make the save. He kicks the ball out of bounds. Whew!

Twenty. I think my hands are dead. But I'm hanging on.

Thirty.

Hey, Rick's not hiccuping any more. I tap him on the shoulder with a dead hand.

"Huh?" He's watching the ball bounce way over onto the baseball field.

I tap him again. "Hey, Rick, you're okay. You're not hiccuping any more."

He just stands there looking lost. Maybe he's really sick or something.

The ref is bringing the ball back.

I shake his shoulder. "Say, Rick, you can go in now."

He blinks. "Yeah. Sure." Very slowly he turns and taps the coach on the shoulder. "Hey, Coach, guess what. I'm not hiccuping any more." It's not like Rick to move so slowly. What's the matter with him?

The coach grabs his shoulder. "Okay, get moving, Ginetti." He waves toward the field. "Get in there. Get going before the throw-in."

The ref is handing the ball to this Penfield High guy with the beard for the throw-in, and Rick isn't moving.

The coach slaps Rick on the back really hard. "Ginetti, will ya *move?*"

It's as if somebody pressed a button. Rick finally jerks himself back to life. He tears over to check in with the timekeeper and rushes into the game. He's okay now.

But I'm exhausted. I collapse on the grass next to Heather and let my breath out very, very slowly.

The guy with the beard throws the ball to another guy, who kicks it in toward our goal. Rick's on top of it. He dribbles it out to the line and kicks it halfway down the field. How about that? Halfway down the field.

Some little guy on our team gets it and moves like lightning. He kicks it toward the Penfield goal till he almost runs into their fullback, and passes it to Jackson. All of a sudden the ball's inside the goal, and the Penfield goalie is wearing this lost look and scratching his head. Jackson's grinning.

What happened? Who cares? We got a goal, and the game's tied. Heather and I cheer and cheer.

After that the guys beat their brains out charging up and down that field, but neither team can make another goal. Coach Boone keeps shaking his head and waving his hands and whispering when he tries to yell. The Hifflicker Hornets have to settle for a tie, but at least they don't get beat.

After the game, Coach Boone comes over to where Heather and I are standing. The sweat is pouring down his face, and he can barely whisper. "Thanks a lot—uh—"

"Carrie. Carrie Mills. I'm Rick's—" I just can't say I'm Rick's sister. It sticks in my throat. "See, my mom's married to Rick's dad."

"Yeah? Well, thanks a lot, Carrie. Rick's one of our most valuable players."

On our way out, Rick catches up to Heather and me. He's breathing hard from the game. Somehow he doesn't look very big any more. "That's some grip you got, Carrie." Very slowly this smile comes over his face. Hey, he's got dimples! He reaches down and gives me this teeny jab on the arm.

Rick, this very valuable player, smiling at me and jabbing me on the arm. Pretty nice.

All of a sudden he gets serious. Worried lines come into his forehead. He clears his throat. "Say—um—Carrie, you—um—won't say anything about this at home, will ya? I mean, hiccups, of all crazy things. You won't say anything, will ya?"

He's embarrassed. This very valuable player is embarrassed about some dumb old hiccups. Hey, this is my big chance to make a deal. I think about that for a minute. "Okay, Rick, I'll lay off you if you lay off me."

"Whadya mean 'lay off you'?"

"You know perfectly well what I mean. Quit stepping on my foot, and quit shoving me around, and quit making nasty cracks."

"Whadya mean nasty cracks?"

"I mean telling Mom she's making you do all the work. And calling me a brat. That kinda stuff."

"Listen, Carrie, you jabbed my ankle and you know it."

I shrug. "Okay, Rick, it's no deal." I take Heather's arm, and we start to walk away.

"Hey, wait a minute." He comes after us. "Okay, okay, I'll cut it out. I wasn't doing anything, but I'll quit."

Heather giggles. "He wasn't doing anything, but he'll quit. That makes a lotta sense."

"All right, cut it out," says Rick. He wipes his forehead with the back of his hand. "Carrie, I'll say this for you. You're a tough little kid."

Little kid! That makes me pretty mad, but I let it pass. I put my hands on my hips. "Is it a deal or isn't it?"

The sweat's trickling down his nose. He nods. "It's a deal."

"Okay. Heather's a witness. And the minute you get nasty I'm gonna spill the whole thing. How you almost blew the game, and how I—"

"Awright, awright. I said it's a deal."

He turns and trots back toward the gym door. His shoulders are sloping way down. I actually almost feel sorry for him.

"You really fixed him," says Heather.

I hope so. He'd better start shaping up fast.

7 ▶ MOM

'You have to miss school Wednesday, Carrie," says Mom, dishing out scrambled eggs. "We're going to go see the lawyer and go to court."

Holy Columbus! It's three weeks already. I was trying to forget.

Newton bites off a hunk of toast and chews. "'Smatter with Carrie? She in some kinda trouble?"

Dominic tips his chair back, pushing his hands against the kitchen table. I wish the chair would fall over. "Carrie's okay. I told ya, Newton, I'm gonna adopt her, and ya gotta go to court to do that."

"How come you gotta adopt her?" says Ginger. "She's already moved in and taken over my room."

Rick starts to laugh, but I give him the eye, and

he quits laughing. "Shut up, Ginger," he says. At least I got one person that's sticking up for me, even if it's only because I blackmailed him. But Ginger's in one of her nasty moods again. I mean, you never can tell how she's going to act from one minute to the next. She frowns at Rick. "I hate brothers." She slams her fork down on her plate.

Dominic leans forward and hits the table with his fist. "You quit that kinda talk, Ginger. We're all gonna be one family, see? We're all gonna love each other. When I adopt Carrie, she'll be a member of this family just like you." His eyes are flashing, and those eyebrows of his are like bushes. Prickly bushes. "Maybe you think if you're mean to Carrie she and her mom'll go away. Well, they're staying. They're staying for good, so you gotta get used to it."

It's about time he got mad at Ginger. How come he never got really mad at her before? All he thinks about is himself. He only wants to adopt me on account of loving Mom. He's married to Mom, and I'm part of the deal. He doesn't care that Ginger gets mean sometimes. He doesn't care that he took Mom away from just being with me. He doesn't care that I want my own dad back. I bet he never even thinks about that. And now he says we're staying for good.

I can't stand him and his muscles and his beer and his black sideburns and his scary, flashing eyes. I wish there was something I could do so he won't adopt me. Maybe I can run away. But I tried that once when I was six. I was going to find my dad, but all I found was this policeman who took me to the police station so Mom could come and get me.

So now what can I do?

I lean forward. "I don't want to get adopted."

There's this complete silence. Everybody stares, especially Dominic. "Whadya mean you don't wanna get adopted?"

"She really doesn't, Dominic," says Mom. "I hated to tell you, but I know it'll be okay when she gets used to it."

"I'll never get used to it."

"Sure you will," says Dominic. "That's right. Sure. You'll get used to it."

The doorbell rings. "There's Mindy," says Ginger. "C'mon, Rick, let's go."

Dominic looks at his watch. "I'm gonna be late." He gets up and kisses Mom and rushes out.

Newton wipes scrambled egg off his face. "Boy-oh-boy, is Mrs. Holbrecher gonna be mad! Wednesday's the day of the math test, and you're gonna miss it."

Nobody listens to me. Nobody cares.

On Wednesday, Mom and I are going to meet Dominic at the lawyer's office at one, but we take the bus downtown in the morning because it's her day off. It's nice being alone with her for once. We shop for a pair of white shoes for her to wear at the office and a new blouse for me. It's red, and it looks pretty good on me, so I guess Ginger didn't give me bum advice.

For lunch we duck into this little restaurant with black tables and a red carpet and sit at the black counter and order sandwiches from this waitress who looks out the window while she's taking our order. "The lawyer's name is Mr. Grimes," says Mom. "He's going to tell us all about what's going to happen in court. We go to court at two."

Ooh boy! I look at the clock on the wall. It's seventeen minutes to one. That means we'll be in court an hour and seventeen minutes from now. In one hour and seventeen minutes my whole life is going to fall apart.

"Mom, what do I have to say to make you see I'm gonna hate getting adopted? Can't you see?"

"You'll get over it, honey."

"That's what you think. Listen, Dominic's no good. He never even fixed my treasure box. He threw away the pieces."

"No, he didn't."

"Well, where are they?"

"I don't know, but—"

"He threw 'em away. Anyway, he scares me. He's got those flashy black eyes and bushy eyebrows."

"Carrie, please! How can you say those things about him? He loves you." Her lower lip begins to tremble. She crunches a potato chip into her mouth, and this teeny piece falls onto the point of her chin just above the dimple.

I reach over and wipe it off. "He does not love me. Anyway, I don't love him. How can you love somebody that's got bushy eyebrows?"

"I do."

"Honestly, Mom? Do you honestly?" How can anybody as old as my mom actually be in love?

"Sure I love him. He's the sweetest, dearest—"

"What about my dad? I bet he's sweet and dear, and you used to love him before you kicked him out."

"I loved him when I married him, but after a while I just felt sorry for him."

"Well, I love him. I feel all achy about him. How come you didn't keep track of him? How come you had to go and marry Dominic and forget about my dad?"

"You're talking too loud, Carrie."

"I don't care."

She puts her hand on my arm. Her voice is kind of shaky. "See, honey, when Dominic adopts you, that means he's got to take care of you. He can't let you starve or anything. That's what the law says."

"I don't care. I don't want to get called Carrie Ginetti. I despise that name. I'd rather starve."

People really are staring. The waitress is glaring at me sideways, but I don't care hardly at all.

"You can be Carolyn Mills Ginetti," says Mom. "I think that sounds sort of nice."

"I don't. Anyway, I can't stand those kids of his. They're all mean and nasty."

"No, they're not. Look, honey, they lost their mom, and it's hard to have a new one. But I really think they're beginning to get used to me, and you too. Especially the boys."

"Well, with Rick it's only because—" I quit just in

time. I can't tell her how I blackmailed Rick. I can't tell her about the hiccups.

"Because what, Carrie?"

"Oh, nothing."

Actually Rick and Newton are a lot nicer to Mom lately. Of course, with Rick it is partly because I blackmailed him, but I think they're both getting to like her the tiniest bit. Maybe because she really listens to them at the dinner table when they talk about soccer and science and stuff. And nobody can keep from liking Mom when she smiles. Nobody but Ginger, I mean.

"It'll take Ginger longer to get used to us," says Mom. "Lots of times girls depend on their mothers a lot. Besides, she and Dominic have always been very close, and then I came along and got in the way."

"Okay, but how come Dominic spoils her like that? How come he always sticks up for her?"

"He doesn't. You know he doesn't. Honestly, Carrie, sometimes I just don't know what to do with you." Her voice is really shaky now.

I got this brick in my stomach.

Mr. Grimes is on the eighteenth floor of this enormous building. Going up in the elevator, I close my eyes and grab my stomach. The office door is made of glass you can't see through, and it's got a pile of names on it. Dominic is sitting just inside the door, and there's this woman with plastic hair typing behind a window, who looks me over and purrs at us to go right in.

Mr. Grimes's office is full of bookcases with enormous books, and Mr. Grimes is tall and red in the face. He's got gray hair and glasses with wire rims. "Well-l, Carolyn," he says, staring at me as if I'm some new kind of modern art. "Well-l."

He takes off his glasses and puts them on again. He gives Dominic this form to fill out and explains that Dominic will have to support me till I'm eighteen. "As Carolyn's father, you'll have the right to tell her what to do, Mr. Ginetti, and to expect her to do it." The brick flips over in my stomach. "Also," says Mr. Grimes, "she'll have the right to inherit from you." He asks how much Dominic makes, plus a lot of other things. Like where's my dad and how old is Dominic and how many rooms there are in our apartment, and Mom and Dominic say they don't know and forty-one and five rooms and a bath. The whole thing sounds really stupid.

Mr. Grimes takes off his glasses and looks at me.

"Carolyn, the judge might ask you some questions too. He may ask how old you are and where you go to school. All you have to do is speak up so he can hear you. All right?"

"Look, Mr. Grimes—"

"Now, can I answer any questions?" He looks at Mom and Dominic.

"How soon does it get to be legal?" says Dominic. "How soon will she really be my girl?"

"In about a month, after her father's rights are terminated."

My father's rights. Hey, I don't like this one bit.

Dominic turns and gives me this glittery smile. "How about that? One month."

I want to throw up. "But, Mr. Grimes, I don't want—"

The phone rings, and Mr. Grimes answers it and talks for a long time while Dominic fills out the form. When Mr. Grimes hangs up, he says, "Now, before we go into court I'll stop off in the sheriff's office for the summons."

Summons? Mom looks puzzled. "What's the summons for?"

"That's for Carolyn. Just a formality. It means she's to appear in court."

I'm feeling more and more trapped. "Listen, Mr. Grimes, I really don't want—"

"All right, let's go," says Mr. Grimes, taking the form from Dominic and pushing his chair out from his desk with this awful scraping noise. He doesn't even hear me. He doesn't care either. They all think they care, but they don't.

In the elevator going down, I grab my stomach again. Outside, I scuff along the sidewalk next to Mom, walking like some kind of zombi, as if I'm walking in my sleep, passing millions of people with faces made out of old newspapers. I blink my eyes to squeeze the tears out.

We go up to the twenty-third floor of this tremendous building that's mostly windows. Mr. Grimes ducks into an office and comes out with this paper that must be the summons. The courtroom is across the hall. There's this big man at the door wearing a badge like a policeman's. The courtroom is the size of my room at school, and it's quiet like some church. Makes me all shivery. There's this big desk at the other end, raised up. That must be where the judge sits. In front of that there's this sort of wall. This stringy-haired lady is sitting behind it, on the right side. Mr. Grimes explains in a whisper that she's the clerk, and the man at the door is the bailiff. Makes no difference to me. Why should I care?

Some benches are inside the door with people sitting on them, whispering to each other. I collapse on one of them between Mom and Dominic, and we sit there for about a million years. My heart's pounding like crazy. In front of us is this couple with a teeny baby.

Finally the bailiff walks up and stands next to the clerk, a door at the back of the room opens, and in walks this man in a black robe. The bailiff tells everybody to stand up, so we all stand. Everybody must hear my heart hammering. The judge goes up and sits behind the bench. He's got wispy blond hair combed across his bald spot. "Mr. and Mrs. Mahoney and Deborah Anne," he says.

The couple in front of us gets up, and this man who must be their lawyer leads them up to the wall and hands some papers to the judge. Mr. Mahoney is holding this baby all wrapped in pink. Mr. Mahoney isn't one bit like Dominic. He's got a neck, a nice long one.

Deborah Anne Mahoney. That's a neat name. Some people have all the luck.

The bailiff gets Mr. and Mrs. Mahoney to raise

their right hands and swear to tell the truth. The judge asks them some questions I can't hear. Deborah Anne's lucky because she doesn't know what's happening to her. I mean, I know for sure that if my own dad knew I was being adopted he wouldn't let it happen. He'd come and take Mom and me away somewhere, and I wouldn't have to sleep in the same room with Ginger or put up with Dominic's smiles, and Mom would have time for me again.

When it's our turn, I want to run out of the courtroom, but I get up and follow the others as if I'd been wound up. We string out along the wall. Dominic and Mom and me and Mr. Grimes. The judge clears his throat. He looks scary. How come he looks so scary? He doesn't even have sideburns. He leans across the desk and says in this very kind voice, "Mr. Ginetti, has your lawyer explained to you the rights and obligations of adoption?"

How can a person talk so nicely when he's doing such a mean thing?

"Yessir." Dominic answers with this big smile, beaming down at Mom. Mom smiles back. You'd think they were getting married all over again. I mean, all they seem to be thinking of is each other. What about me? Listen, everybody, what about me? Nobody's been listening to me.

They all got bugs in their ears. Enormous big bugs.

The judge turns to me. "How old are you, Carolyn?" he says in his kind voice, pronouncing the words carefully, as if I'm deaf.

"I'm thirteen." How come he's asking these dumb questions? Can't he read? It's got to be on those papers somewhere. And I just know that any minute he's going to say he'll sign the adoption papers.

"Are you living with Dominic and Marie Ginetti?"

"Yes. I—" Now's my chance to say something. Why can't I say it? If I don't say it, I'll bust wide open.

"In that case, the court—"

"Listen, Judge! You gotta listen. Please don't let him adopt me. I want my own dad. Please find my own dad so I can have him back. PLEASE—JUDGE—DON'T—LET—HIM—ADOPT—ME!"

The judge stares. Stringyhair stares. The bailiff stares. Mr. Grimes stares. Dominic and Mom stare. There's this complete silence.

After a long time the judge says to Mr. Grimes, "You say that Carolyn's father has disappeared?"

"That's right, your honor. I believe he—he had a drinking problem. Carolyn doesn't remember him. He moved out when she was just under a year old, and her mother divorced him."

"I do too remember him. He's kind and gentle, and he can take care of me." I'm crying now. "He will, too. I just know he will."

The judge leans farther across his desk. "Carolyn, did he take care of you when you were a baby?"

"Well, no. But he would've done it if—if—"

"And is Mr. Ginetti taking good care of you?"

"Well, there were a couple of times when—"

"When what, Carolyn? Tell me. Did he mistreat you? Did he harm you?"

"Well, n—no." What else can I say?

"You're sure, Carolyn?"

I nod weakly. I sniffle. Mom hands me this tissue.

The judge's voice gets quiet. "You're very fortunate, Carolyn, that he wants to be a father to you. Many children have no father at all." He leans back in his chair. "Carolyn, I'm going to proceed with the adoption, and I feel sure you'll eventually come to understand how lucky you are."

Lucky. Holy Columbus! I can't see the judge

through my tears, but still I want to climb over the wall and sock him. I want to explode and splatter all over him.

Worms are crawling inside my stomach, and Mom has to lead me out of the courtroom. She doesn't say anything. Nobody says anything. On the way home in Dominic's car I feel worse and worse, and when we get to the apartment I just barely make it to the bathroom to throw up.

8 ▶ DOMINIC

I stay home from school the rest of the week. I'm going to die for sure. Ginger moves onto the sofa bed in the living room to get away from my fatal germs, and Mom brings me a saucepan to throw up in.

On Saturday morning I miss swimming at the Y, but that's okay because I can swim at the deep end now. In case I ever get well and some boat tips over under me, I could save myself.

Around breakfast time, Ginger sneaks into the room and grabs jeans and stuff to wear over to Mindy's. I hear Mom go out to work. Rick must have gone to soccer practice because I heard him asking Newt where his clean sweat socks were.

106 ▶ DOMINIC

Newt goes out too. "I'll be over at Stafford's, Dad," he yells. That leaves me home alone with Dominic.

I turn over and go back to sleep.

I wake up around ten-thirty. I have to go to the bathroom. I'm all weak and gloppy, but I feel around for my robe and slippers and shuffle through the living room. Dominic's not there. I pad down the hall, trying to be quiet so he won't know I'm up. In the bathroom I decide I really don't have to throw up. Well, that's a change anyway. Maybe I'm going to live after all. I start brushing my teeth.

Maybe I don't want to live, though. Maybe I really want to die. I mean, am I going to have to go on like this forever? With Ginger writing things in her diary. Horrible things, I bet, and they're all about me, of course. Wish I could see what she's got in there. And Dominic. That dumb way he always looks at Mom makes me feel—well, let's face it. It makes me feel left out.

I examine my teeth in the mirror. They look okay. Maybe I'm glad I didn't die. Maybe Dominic's not all that bad. Anyway, I'm stuck with him, and he does smile at me a lot, and he wants to support me, and he's got this really gorgeous voice.

Can I ever get used to him even though he does sweat, and even though he always makes me feel little?

Right now I'm hungry. Maybe I can even eat something. Mom always gives me clear soup when I've been sick. Maybe I can find a bouillon cube in the kitchen somewhere.

I stop in the kitchen doorway. Ooh boy! There's Dominic at the kitchen table. He's stirring this cup of coffee very slowly. He doesn't see me. Maybe I can sneak back to my room without making any noise. I start to turn around. He looks up. He doesn't smile. His eyes aren't shining. He's got gloom lines going down his cheeks. He keeps right on stirring, round and round.

He's got to be mad at me.

"You feel better, Carrie?"

"Uh huh. A little. I thought maybe I'd get some soup or something. Maybe some bouillon."

"Sure. You come on in and sit down. I'll get some bouillon cubes. They gotta be around somewhere."

I go in very slowly. How come he doesn't bawl me out? How come he doesn't get it over with?

He gets up and yanks open the door of one of the

bottom cupboards and rummages around and pulls out this teeny bottle. The label is kind of gray, and when he pulls out a bouillon cube, the paper sticks to it. It must be a hundred years old. It must be left over from when Ginger's mom was alive.

He turns on the stove under the hot water kettle. "So you feel better, Carrie. That's nice." He's fixing soup for me, and he hasn't bawled me out, and his coffee's getting cold.

He comes and sits down across from me. Now he'll bawl me out. But he doesn't. He looks down at the coffee and doesn't say anything. I can't think of anything to say either. I mean, do I say I wish I wasn't here? I wish I was living at the zoo, or the art museum, or in some orphanage somewhere? Dominic sips his coffee, and after a while all that silence gets plenty embarrassing. Seems funny for him to be this way. I've never seen him when he doesn't have something to say. He must be plenty mad.

When the water boils, he gets up and fixes the bouillon and brings it over and sets it down in front of me.

"Thanks, Dominic."

He sits down. He clears his throat and says in this

very quiet voice, "Listen, Carrie, I'm sorry you don't like it here with me. Tell me if there's something I can do to make it better for you. Tell me, what can I do, Carrie?"

He didn't bawl me out.

I don't know what to say. I just don't know what to say. I look at the window, at his hands grabbing the cup of coffee, at the counter behind him, trying to think.

Hey! On the counter behind him. That's—that's my treasure box! It's all whole, just the way it was before. I can't even see any cracks in it.

Dominic sees I'm staring. He turns and picks up the box very gently and sets it on the table. "I took the old finish off and put a new coat on. Nice, huh?"

"Yeah."

His eyes begin to sparkle. "I was gonna give it to you the other day after we got home from court. I had it all ready for a surprise. Even your mom didn't know about it. I did it on Saturdays while she was at work." He gives me this sort of shy look, as if maybe he's scared of me, as if he's scared I might not like it. I never knew he could be scared, especially of me.

"It's—it's gorgeous, Dominic."

He smiles. "Bet you thought I forgot about it, huh?"

"Yeah. I really did, y'know. I thought you threw it away."

"Threw it away? How could I throw it away? Beautiful box like this. Carrie, listen. I know this box is special. Right?"

"Yeah. Right."

He pushes his cup away and rests his arms against the table and gets the sad look on his face again. "You miss your dad, huh?"

I nod. I never guessed he thought about that.

"Sure you miss him, honey. Why not?"

Why not? He says why not. I take a sip of the bouillon, and it feels warm. Funny. Dominic's eyes are warm too.

"See, I worry about my dad. I hope he's okay. I hope he's not in any trouble."

"He's probably okay. I wouldn't be surprised."

"And I wonder sometimes. I wonder if he even remembers me."

What's going on with me? I never talked like this to anybody before. Not even to Mom.

"Sure he remembers you. Sure, Carrie." He looks away. "If I ever got separated from Ginger, if I ever had to leave her—well—I'd remember. Sure I would."

Guess that's right. No wonder he thinks so much of Ginger. She's his own daughter. How come I never thought about that?

"Don't worry, Carrie. Your dad didn't forget you."

"Sometimes—sometimes I think he's dead. D'you think he's dead, Dominic?"

"Maybe. Maybe not. It's not the worst thing that can happen, y'know." He looks at me a long time. "Listen, you gotta stop thinking those things, 'cause it won't help. It's better if you start new. You gotta make yourself start all over again 'cause now you're Carrie Ginetti."

Carrie Ginetti, Carrie Ginetti, Carrie Ginetti. It's like being in this dream, and I got to get used to the dream.

We talk for a long time, and we laugh some, and after a while I don't feel scared any more.

"I had this box," he says. "When I was a kid, I had this box like yours. Only it was one of my old man's cigar boxes. Smelled like stale salami." He laughs. "The stuff I used to keep in that thing. Match covers. And used stamps. I was always gonna collect stamps. Bottle tops, too. I even had this dead beetle in there. It fell apart after a while, and there were pieces of it all through my stuff."

I never thought about Dominic saving match covers and pieces of beetle. I never thought about Dominic being a kid.

"Did ya know?" he says after a while. "Your mom and me, we'll be married two months soon. A week from Wednesday it'll be two months."

"Yeah? Hey, you really oughta celebrate. Maybe go out for dinner or something." It comes to me that Dominic and Mom really deserve to have some fun. I mean, this last couple of months has been pretty tough on both of them, I guess.

Dominic pushes his chair back. "I'll wash up. You go get some rest, honey."

I pick up the treasure box. "Thanks, Dominic."

In my room I take my treasures out from under my socks and put them in the box. The ticket stub from *Our Town*. This report card from first grade, all wadded up. A picture of me and Aunt Angie, Mom's sister, out in front of Mr. Flugum's plumbing shop when she came to visit. A poem I wrote about airplanes flying over buildings. The silver dollar from Grandma. There's even this match cover from some place called Bernie's Bar that I picked up off the sidewalk last summer.

A match cover. I forgot all about that.

9 ▶ THE FAMILY

"I've got this idea, Newt."

"Yeah? So what's your great idea, Carrie?"

It's Sunday afternoon, and Newt's lying on his bed reading *Commodore Hornblower*.

"First, have you got any money?"

"Listen, I'm in the most exciting part. The part where he's trying to trap the French fleet and he's being accidentally fired on by one of his own ships, and you come in here and tell me you got this fantastic idea and ask if I've got any money. Well, I don't."

"Aw, c'mon, Newt. You gotta have money. You buy all kinds of stuff for Freckles."

He squints at me. "Spill it, Carrie. What's it for?"

I settle down on Rick's bed with my legs out in front of me. "We're gonna take Mom and Dominic out to dinner next Wednesday. It's their anniversary."

"Whadya mean? They haven't been married a year."

For a bright kid, he can be pretty dumb. "It's their two-months anniversary."

"You crazy or something?" He sticks his nose back in the book.

"Newt, please! Listen, this anniversary means a whole lot to Dominic. Honestly. He told me."

His eyelids flicker. "Yeah?" I must be getting to him.

"See, Newt, I guess these things are more important when you first get married."

"Well, thank goodness we don't have to do this every two months for the rest of their lives. We'd all go broke."

"You got some money, don't you?"

"Well-l. What I meant was I haven't got any money that's extra. I'm saving up for plants for Freckles's cage, y'know."

"How much you got?"

"Three bucks, maybe." He turns the page.

Rick wanders in, and I ask him how much money he's got.

"For what?"

"We're taking Mom and Dominic out to dinner."

"Sez who?"

"Sez me. Newt thinks it's a great idea, don't you, Newt?"

Newt shrugs with his nose in the book. "Not bad."

I really got to him.

Rick lies on the floor and starts doing push-ups.

"It's for their anniversary, Rick. Their two-months anniversary. We're all gonna chip in. We could go to Gino's. That's where they got engaged."

Rick is counting. "Five, six. Not a bad idea. Your mom's okay. But Ginger'll never go for it. Nine, ten, eleven . . ."

"I was sort of counting on you guys to ask her. If I ask her, she won't do it. But maybe you could just tell her we're all going out to dinner. Period. It's three against one."

"Naw," says Newt. "She'd never chip in. Look, you guys, we gotta trick her into it."

"Right," says Rick. "There's only one way to get her money. Twenty-two, twenty-three. Get her diary."

"Whadya mean, get her diary?" says Newt.

"Steal it."

"Steal it? But that's a low-down, dirty—Well, maybe it's not such a low-down, dirty trick. It's for a good cause."

"Sure. Tell her we'll jimmy the lock if she doesn't kick in." Rick stops the push-ups. "Now I lost my count."

I'm worried. "But we only jimmy the lock if she absolutely refuses. Right?"

"Right," says Rick, turning over on his back. "Get the diary, Carrie." He starts doing sit-ups.

"Me? Get the diary?"

"Get the diary," says Newt, turning another page.

"Listen, you guys, I'm not gonna do that. See, she gave me some really great advice about clothes and stuff. Anyway, she'd kill me."

Newt looks up. "I know exactly how you feel. But you gotta fight fire with fire. Rick's right. If you don't do it, the whole thing's gonna fall through. Dya want that to happen?"

"Well, no."

"I thought you could do anything, Carrie," says Rick from the floor.

That does it.

On Saturday afternoon, while Ginger's at the movies with Mindy, I slip the diary out from under her mattress. I sneak it into the boys' room and hand it to Newt. "Okay. When she misses it, I'm gonna tell her I gave it to you guys. After that you gotta do the talking."

"That's fair. You got the diary. We'll do the talking."

That night she goes to some party, so I guess she's too tired to write in her diary when she gets home. But the next night the suspense is over. She reaches under the mattress and feels all around while I try to pretend I don't notice. "Hey, what happened to my diary?"

"I took it."

"You—you took it? You actually took it? Why, you sneaky little—You give it back or I'll kill you, you—"

"Don't kill me. See, I gave it to Rick and Newt."

"Rick and Newt?" She's just about screaming. "You gave it to those—those boys?"

"They haven't opened it. Honest."

"Whadya mean they haven't opened it? I'll bet they ripped it open. Ooh, that's a low-down, dirty—"

"Ginger, please! Please go talk to the guys. They'll explain everything."

"They'd better."

She whizzes out of the room and I follow her. She rips open the door of the boys' room and walks right in, with me after her. Rick's studying at the desk, and Newt's standing in the middle of the room in his underpants. "Hey, Ginger, what's the big idea?"

"Now listen, you guys. Whadya mean by getting that little brat to steal my diary? It's private, see? You give me back my diary or I'll—"

"Simmer down, Ginger," say Newt.

"I will not. I want to know what—"

"Simmer down, Ginger," says Rick, glaring.

She glares back.

"We'll give it back," says Rick. "We haven't opened it. Not yet. So sit down."

She sits. "You better give me a good explanation for this."

"So shut up," says Rick. "First, how much money you got?"

"Y'mean I gotta pay money to get back my diary? That's the worst—"

"The money's not to get back your diary. It's to help pay for the meal we're giving Dad and Marie. We're all taking them out to dinner this Wednesday."

"Well, I'm staying out of it. I'm not going to help with a goofy idea like that."

"Okay. No money, no diary."

"Oooh! You guys make me mad!"

"Take it or leave it."

"I bet I could find that diary. It's gotta be in this room someplace."

"Be our guest," says Rick, pushing his chair back and crossing his legs.

She gets up and looks through the desk drawers, under the bureau and the beds, and in the closet. Where is that diary anyway? Finally she gives up. She sits down and drums her fingers on the arm of the chair and snaps her gum.

"How much money you got?" says Rick.

"A quarter."

"That's not enough."

"That's all I got."

"It's not enough."

"Okay. Fifty cents."

"It'll take three dollars."

"Three dollars! That's blackmail. That's just plain blackmail, y'know."

"That's what it'll take. I know you been saving up for next year's diary."

"So now I won't be able to get it."

"There's no hurry. You'll get it before January if you skip lunch a few times."

"Listen, Ginger," says Newt, "it's almost two months since Dad and Marie got married. So we're gonna surprise 'em, see? We're all gonna chip in."

"That's a dumb thing to celebrate."

"Maybe," says Rick. "Maybe it's not so easy to get used to. It's like chicken pox. But when you got 'em you might as well get used to 'em."

"Marie's been pretty nice to us kids," says Newt.

"And Carrie can't help it if she's gotta share your room," says Rick.

"She told us you gave her some good advice about clothes and stuff," says Newt.

"She told you that?" Ginger looks at me as if I'm an actual human being.

"C'mon, Ginger." Newt leans over so his head almost touches hers. His thumbs pull the skin down under his eyes so his eyeballs are skinned and the red parts show.

She laughs. "Don't be gruesome, Newton."

"Will ya go along with us?"

"Oh, all right."

Rick pulls her diary out of his pile of school books and hands it to her. It was right there on his desk the whole time.

That night I count the money in my top drawer. I was saving it from my baby-sitting money for Christmas presents, but I don't care. There's only two dollars and twenty-three cents.

I open the treasure box and get out the silver dollar, the one I was planning to keep forever. I turn it over and over in my hand. I hate to use it. But I think Grandma'd want me to. Didn't she say you've got to be ready for everything? And she said the silver dollar might bring me luck. Anyway, I don't need any dumb old piece of money to remember her by.

Ginger's watching me. "Hey, Carrie, is that the silver dollar you said you got from your grandma?"

"Yeah."

"You gonna use it to chip in for the dinner?"

I nod.

"You shouldn't use that. You should save it. It's special."

"Well, I'm gonna use it."

She gives me this long, surprised look, and then she slowly reaches under the mattress and gets out her diary and starts writing.

I'm getting more and more curious about that diary.

When Dominic comes home on Wednesday, Rick tells him and Mom we're taking them to Gino's for pizza.

Mom gets all sniffly.

Dominic smiles. "That's real nice of you kids. You're good kids." He's got dimples just like Rick's. How come I never noticed?

I wear my new red blouse to Gino's. "You look good in that blouse," says Ginger. "It's nice."

I've never been to an Italian restaurant before. The place mats in the booth have a picture of this man wearing a chef's hat. He's got this mustache that goes down to his chin, and black eyes like Dominic's. In fact, he looks like Dominic except for the mustache.

Mom smiles a lot, and Dominic puts his arm around her and hugs her and tells her she's beautiful. He looks around at all of us and smiles his shiny smile. For some reason it doesn't bother me. I guess I don't feel so left out any more.

"We got a good family, Marie," says Dominic.

"Sure," says Mom. "We got a really good family."

"We're all gonna love each other," says Dominic.

We all giggle. Even Ginger. We all start talking at once. People all around us are smiling.

The waiter brings wine for Dominic and Mom and soft drinks for us kids. When he brings the pizzas, everybody starts grabbing a piece of each kind and shoving bites into their mouths. I grab Rick's arm, next to me. "Hey, how's about letting me have some?"

He gives me this surprised look. "Y'mean you didn't get any? Okay. Here's some anchovy pizza." He picks up this hunk with teeny little fish all over it and plunks it on my plate. Everybody watches me take my first bite. Wow! It's hot. I almost spit it out. My face must be beet red. Everybody laughs, but I keep chewing.

"Good girl, Carrie," says Rick.

"Hey, you're gonna be some Italiano," says Dominic.

"An honest-to-gosh Ginetti," says Newt.

"That's for sure," says Ginger.

Mom just beams.

I get this sort of glowing feeling. I'm part of the family now, and it's not so bad.

When it's time for dessert, Rick says, "Let's all have spumoni. C'mon, everybody. Let's all have— Hey, Newt, quit kicking me."

There's this absolute silence. Rick hasn't bothered to add up how much money we spent on the drinks and pizza, and it's almost our whole twelve dollars. We don't have enough for dessert, and this has got to be why Newt is kicking him.

"We don't want any dessert, Rick," says Newt in a loud voice. "We're all full. Right, Rick?"

Rick finally catches on. "Oh, yeah. Right. We don't want any dessert."

I do. I'm still hungry. Everybody else looks hungry too. Everybody looks disappointed, but nobody says anything.

Dominic laughs. "It's okay, kids. I'll pay for the dessert. We're all gonna be happy, right?"

I never ate spumoni before, but it turns out to be pretty good. All creamy and smooth. And it's got nuts in it and cherries. I might get used to this Italian food some day. Everybody's talking and laughing, and all of a sudden the wine's gone, the soft drinks are gone, the spumoni's gone, everything's gone. I fold up my place mat and stick it in my pocket. It's only got this teeny bit of spumoni spilled on it.

At the door, Dominic and Rick pay the cashier. Dominic turns around and hugs everybody, one after the other. I'm last. Funny. It feels good getting hugged by Dominic. It feels warm and safe.

Everybody hugs everybody. Mom hugs Ginger first, and then she stands there with her hands on Ginger's arms and smiles. Ginger smiles back, this sort of surprised smile. Mom hugs the rest of us, ending up with Dominic, and everybody's laughing. Even the cashier. Even the other customers.

That night while Ginger's writing in her diary, the phone rings. Mom calls from the living room. "It's for you, Ginger. It's Mindy." Ginger leaves her diary spread out upside down on her bed and goes out. I can't resist. "October 26," it says. "All of us went to Gino's for pizza and spumoni. It was Carrie's idea, and it turned out really nice. I'm going to try to be—" That's where it stops.

She's going to try being friends with me, I just know. Maybe she's finally getting used to me.

Maybe now she's not missing her own mom the way she did before.

I'm dying to read more, but she might come back any minute. I put the diary back on her bed and get out the place mat from Gino's and unfold it and smooth it out. Except for the mustache and the spot of spumoni on his cheek, the man in the picture really does look like Dominic. I open my treasure box on the bureau and look through my treasures. Funny. I never thought about it before, but there's nothing here to remind me of my dad. I guess he never gave me anything.

I fold the place mat again and put it into the box on top of my other treasures. I close the box and slide the secret panel into its place. I run my fingers over the top of the box. It's all smooth and shiny, and I can hardly feel the cracks where Dominic fixed them.